FIRST DAY CRITTER JITTERS

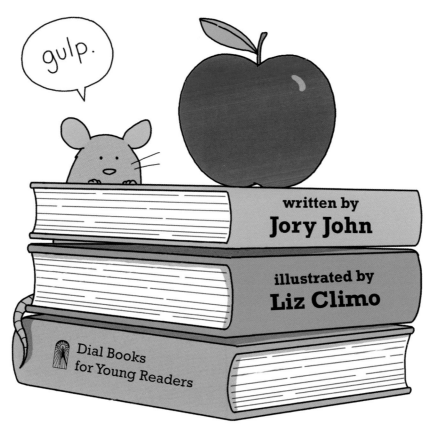

gulp.

written by
Jory John

illustrated by
Liz Climo

Dial Books
for Young Readers

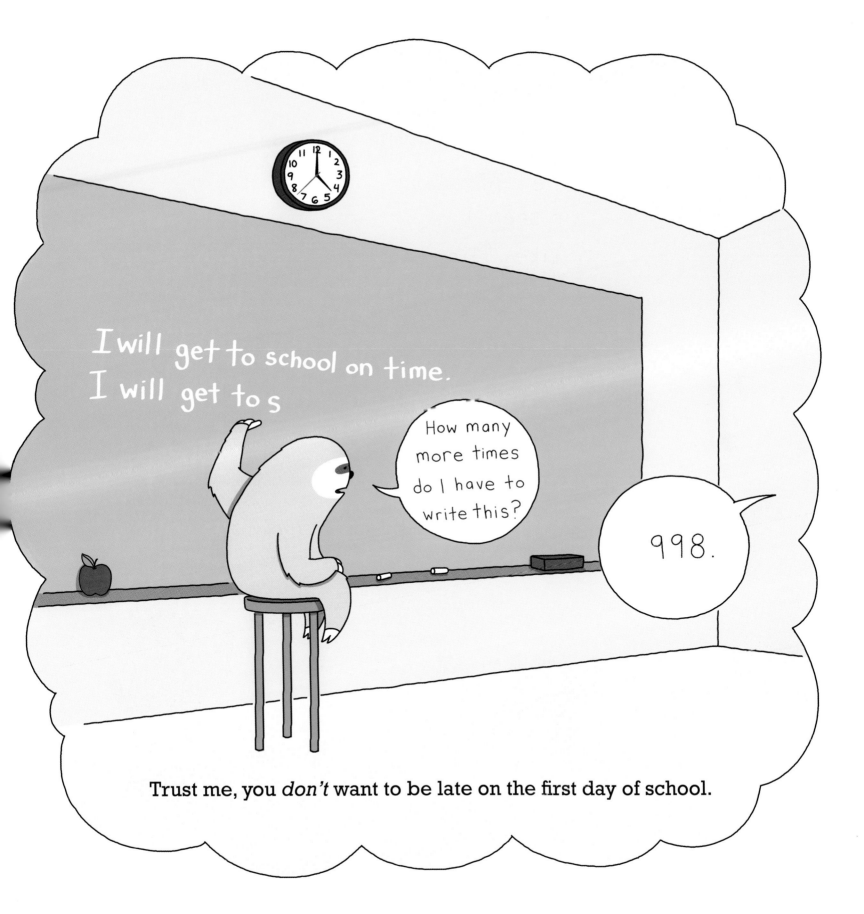

Trust me, you *don't* want to be late on the first day of school.

Maybe next year I'll be ready.

I have a feeling that's not going to fly at school.

So, yeah...I've already been traveling toward the bus stop for twenty minutes and I'm still at my front door. I should really learn how to ride a bike. Sheesh.

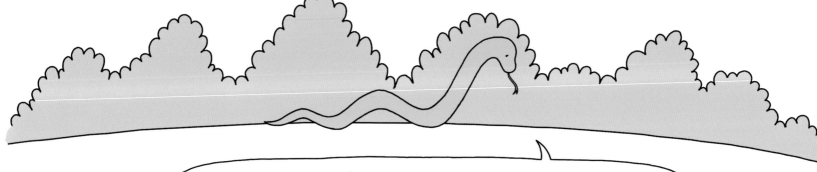

Bye-bye, backpack. Sniff. Bye-bye, lunch. Sniff. Bye-bye, art supplies. Sniff.

I'm exhausted. Aren't I supposed to be hibernating right now?

...can't stop hopping, so much energy, can't stop hopping, so much energy, can't stop hopping, so much...

My eyelids... won't... stop... closing...

...I'm almost to the sidewalk... I can do this... just a few more blocks to go... yes... feel the burn...

Right now, my mom and I would be reading a book together and drinking hot chocolate with marshmallows. Do buses have hot chocolate?

Ah, well, yes. I feel a bit silly about this, but I have *plenty* to be nervous about. The truth is, I'm rather forgetful. What if I can't remember all of your names? What if I forget the last thing I said? What if I can't recall where I put the chalk?

Don't worry, Mr. Sherwood! I may be a tiny mouse, but I have the memory of an *elephant!* And I'll help you remember our names using a mnemonic device! For example, my name is *Chauncy* and I like *cheese*. See how that works?

munch
munch
munch

The next day . . .

To Alyssa, of course —J.J.

For Kathleen —L.C.

Dial Books for Young Readers
An imprint of Penguin Random House LLC, New York

Text copyright © 2020 by Jory John
Illustrations copyright © 2020 by Liz Climo

Visit us online at penguinrandomhouse.com

Library of Congress Cataloging-in-Publication Data is available.

Manufactured in Italy • LEG • ISBN 9780593616024

1 3 5 7 9 10 8 6 4 2

Design by Lily Malcom • Text handlettered and set in Rockwell

The illustrations in the book were done with digital magic.